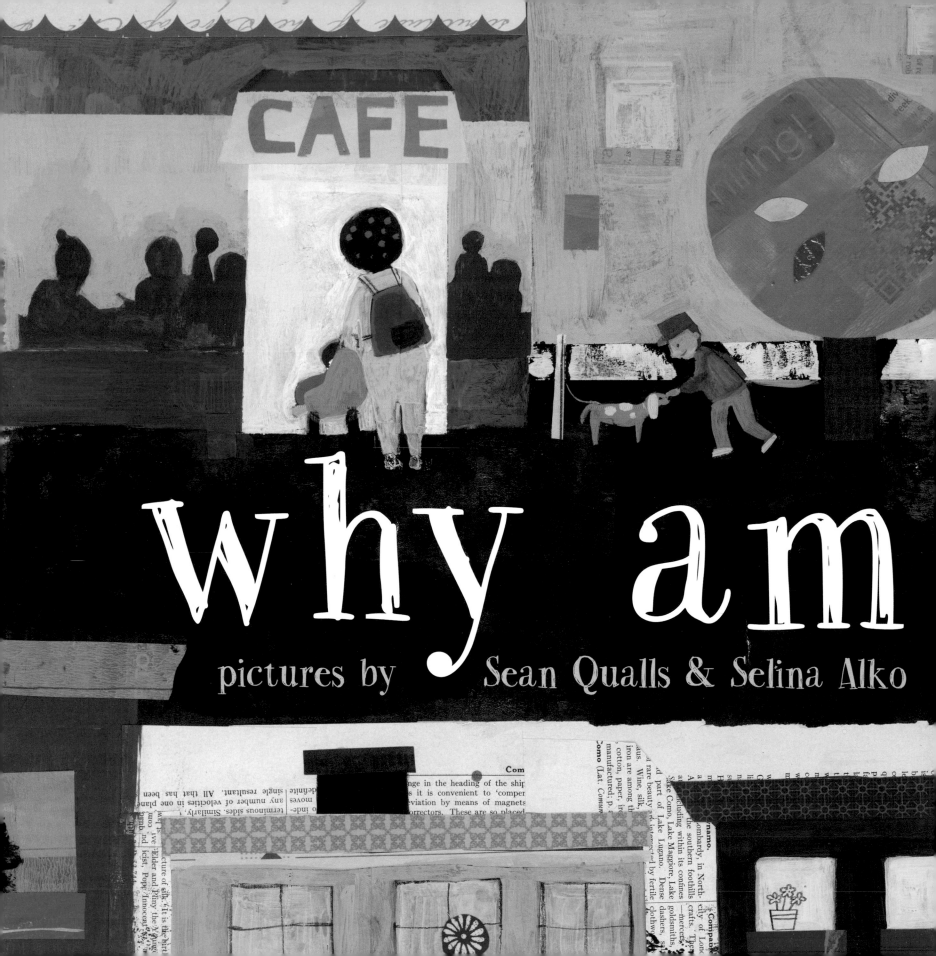

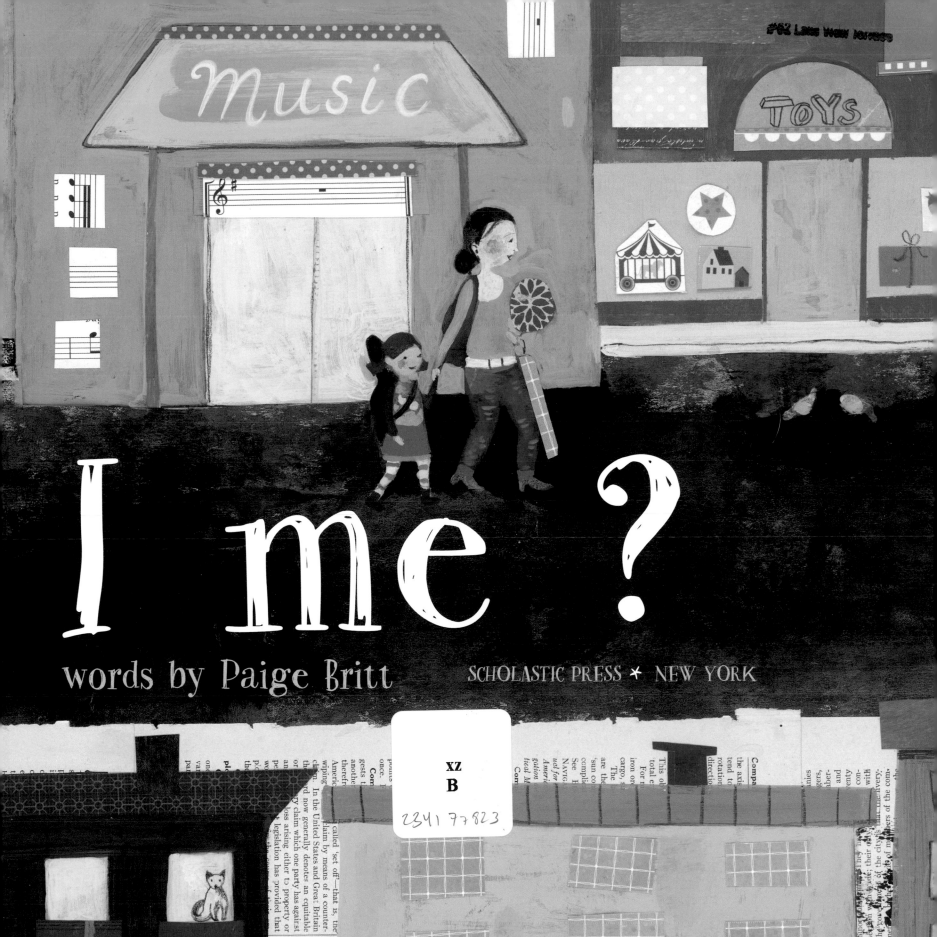

I me ?

words by Paige Britt

SCHOLASTIC PRESS ✶ NEW YORK

LIBRARY OF CONGRESS CATALOG CARD NUMBER: 2016045588
ISBN 978-1-338-05314-2 · 10 9 8 7 6 5 4 3 2 1   17 18 19 20 21
Printed in the U.S.A 88 · First edition, September 2017
The art was created using acrylic paint, colored pencil, and collage.
The text and display type were set in Two Fingers Bodoni.
Art direction and book design by Marijka Kostiw

To Peg Syverson and Flint Sparks,
for extending the invitation
to see and be seen. —P.B.

To Ginger and Isaiah,
you are our future. —S.Q.

To Sean,
with everlasting wonder. —S.A.

. . . and not

someone else entirely?

If I were someone else,

who would I be?

Someone taller,

faster,

smaller,

smarter?

Someone lighter,
older,

Why . . .

am . . .

. . . . . me?

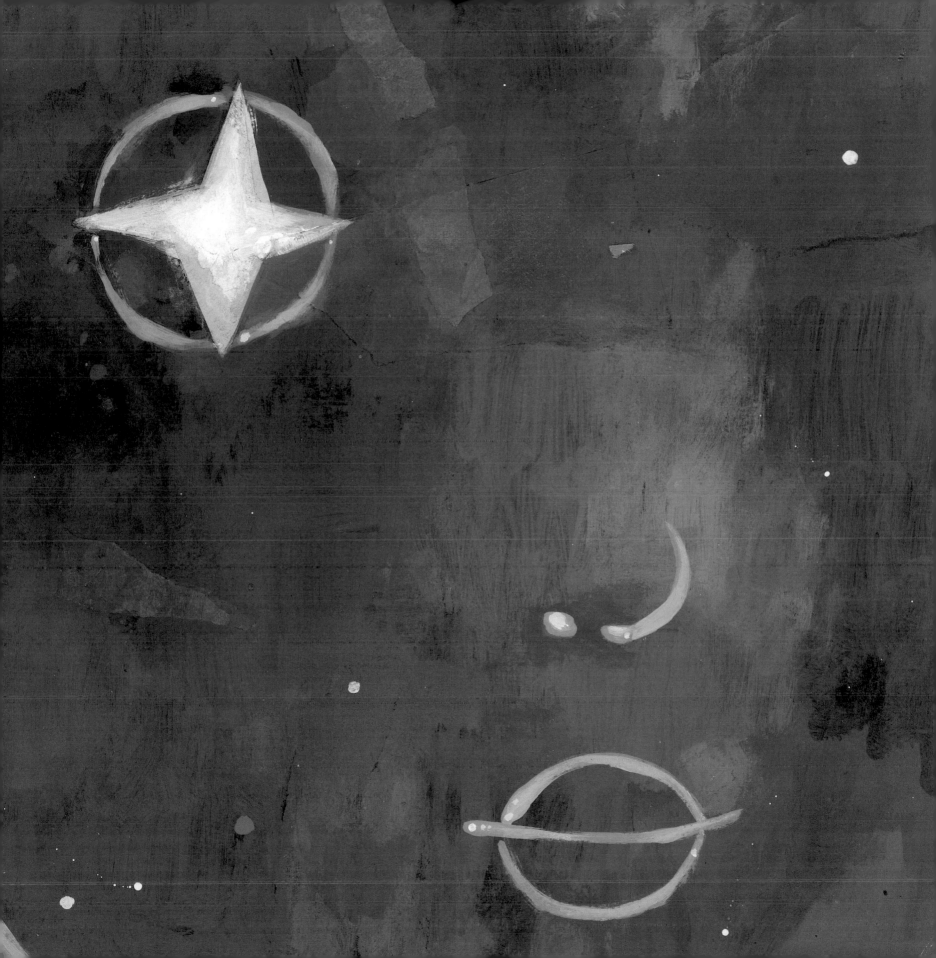

Why . . .

am . . .

. . . . . me?

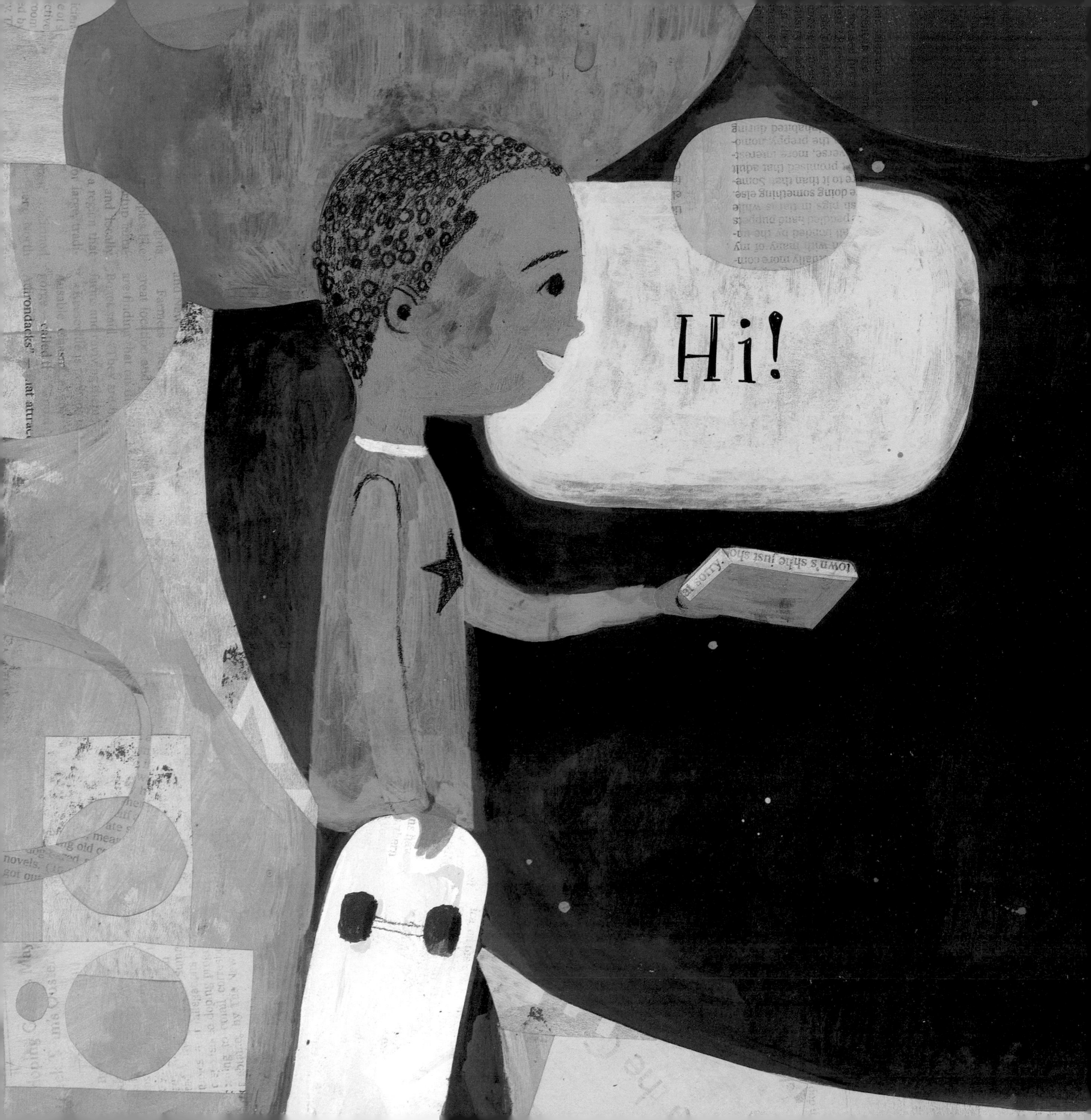
Hi!

me

I

you

I

you

me

we

I

me

you